PATRICIA ST JOHN

Friska My Friend

Copyright © Patricia St John 1983
This edition revised 2007
Reprinted 2011

ISBN 978 1 84427 289 1

Scripture Union
207–209 Queensway, Bletchley, Milton Keynes, MK2 2EB, England
Email: info@scriptureunion.org.uk
Website: www.scriptureunion.org.uk

Scripture Union Australia
Locked Bag 2, Central Coast Business Centre, NSW 2252
Website: www.scriptureunion.org.au

Scripture Union USA
PO Box 987, Valley Forge, PA 19482
Website: www.scriptureunion.org

The right of Patricia St John to be identified as author of this work has been
asserted by her in accordance with the Copyright, Designs and Patents Act 1988.

British Library Cataloguing-in-Publication Data.
A catalogue record of this book is available from the British Library.

Printed and bound in India by Nutech Print Services

Cover design by Go Ballistic
Internal design and layout by Author and Publisher Services

Scripture Union is an international Christian charity working with churches in
more than 130 countries, providing resources to bring the good news about Jesus
Christ to children, young people and families and to encourage them to develop
spiritually through the Bible and prayer.

As well as our network of volunteers, staff and associates who run holidays,
church-based events and school Christian groups, we produce a wide range
of publications and support those who use our resources through training
programmes.

Chapter one

It was half past three. And on that warm, sunny afternoon in early summer, the children were glad to get out of school. They ran across the playground, pushing and jostling out through the gate. Some jumped into waiting cars but most of them turned down the road that led to the village. Colin went with them, but where the road split in two he stopped and his friend Will stopped too.

"Here," said Will, fishing in his school bag, "I've got something for her. My mum said I could have the leftovers." And he pushed something wrapped in greaseproof paper into Colin's hand.

"Thanks," said Colin. "Coming to see her?"

Will shook his head.

"Not now. We're going down to Gran's for tea. Mum said I was to come straight home. Maybe I'll come tomorrow. But, Cal, my dad said we've got to do something or tell someone. We can't just keep on giving her things. What'll happen when we go to camp?"

"That's ages yet."

"Yes, but —"

Colin stuffed the greaseproof paper into his bag with his school books and nodded. "I'll tell my dad tonight," he said. "He'll know what to do. I wish... oh, I do wish..."

"What d'you wish?"

"That I could have her," said Colin. "I just wish that she was mine. I'd soon fatten her up."

Will nodded. "I might bring a sausage from Gran's," he said comfortingly. "She always gives us sausages! Bye, Cal, see you." He ran off down the road. Colin crossed to the lane that led up the hillside toward his home. He was quite glad to be alone because he had a lot to think about. It was a beautiful day and late bluebells and buttercups grew along the hedge. The warm sun shone on his face and from somewhere in the oak wood a cuckoo called. Then he turned off the lane and climbed a little track that led to the common beyond. On the edge of the common was a cottage surrounded by a garden.

The garden gate was broken and the paint was cracked. Colin rested his chin on it and looked round. The garden was choked with weeds. The grass had grown

as high as his knees. The windows of the cottage were dirty and tight shut. Colin gave a soft whistle.

Nothing happened.

Colin whistled quite loudly with his eye on the window.

There was a sudden rush. A black dog, half Labrador and half terrier, came streaking round the side of the house. She was barking excitedly. She put her paws on the bottom bars of the gate and pushed her nose through the gap. Her whole thin body shook with excitement. Colin pulled the greaseproof paper parcel out of his bag. He fed the dog with half a Cornish pasty and a piece of cheese. He also had some ham, broken bread and crackers from his lunchbox. He stuck his hand

through the bars and stroked the thin dog. He could count every rib. The dog nosed his face, licked his cheeks and whined with pleasure.

"Don't go," she seemed to be saying. "Please don't go. I need you so much."

Colin stayed quite a long time, stroking and patting the dog. He spoke to her softly because she seemed to understand.

"I'm going to talk to my Dad about you," said Colin. "I'm going to do something. I wish you were mine. I'd soon fatten you up and you'd be the best dog in the village. But I don't suppose Dad would let me keep you. We've got Growler already on the farm. He's our guard dog. He's not nice and friendly like you."

He left at last, turning back and waving at the twitching black nose poked through the bars. Then the track turned into the wood and he could no longer hear the short, sharp little barks. He felt very unhappy even though he had promised to go back tomorrow. He did not know who lived in that cottage. But he did know that someone was starving the dog. He hurried up the lane and into the farmyard at the top of the hill. He was home.

He liked living at the top of the hill. If he looked behind him, he could see the north end of the hills rising steeply behind his school. On the other side, the meadows sloped gently to the woods, hop fields and blossoming orchards of Worcestershire. It was like being on top of the world, thought Colin, as he trotted across the yard. He went straight to the milking shed. He was quite late and Dad would be busy with the cows. Colin pushed past the orderly herd that stood waiting their turn outside. He went into the big shed.

His father, in his white coat, was fastening the nozzles on the udders of the cows. The electric siphon was whining and the milk was sloshing in the tank. The cows mooed contentedly. It was quite noisy.

"Dad!" shouted Colin, standing on tiptoe. "There's a dog and she's very thin—"

"What's that?" asked Dad, stooping down. "Dog? The dog's all right, Colin. I've just fed him. Run in and tell Mum I'll be along in about half an hour."

Colin sighed. It was no good trying to talk to Dad during the milking. Perhaps Mum would help. He ran over to the house and found Mum putting a big shepherd's pie in the oven. His sister, Joy, had just come in from her school.

"Mum," said Colin, "there's a poor dog and she's very, very thin. She might be starving."

"Then we'd best call the RSPCA. They care for animals that have been badly treated, don't they? Who does this dog belong to, Colin?"

"I don't know. It's a cottage and it looks all shut up."

"If she's starving, the RSPCA'll come and take her. Go and change, Colin, and then you can collect the eggs."

About half an hour later they all sat down to their tea and Colin started again. "Dad, there's a dog, and she's very thin, almost starving. How do I get the RSPCA to come out to her?"

"Well, you'd best find out who she belongs to first. Where did you see her?"

"Will and I went up the common to look for nests last week. There's a cottage at the edge of the common. It's all untidy and shut up. Dad, the dog's ever so thin."

His father looked interested. "That'll be old Charlie's cottage," he said. "He went to live there after his wife died. Strange old man, they say he is. Won't let anyone into his house. But that dog was his best friend. Old Charlie would never mistreat his dog. There must be something wrong. Why didn't you tell us before?"

"It was a sort of secret and we thought we'd feed her ourselves. Then we suddenly thought, maybe there's no one there and we'd best tell."

"Perhaps old Charlie's ill or something," said Mum. "Someone ought to call in. Maybe we'd better call the police."

"Well, he might not like that," said Dad. "How about asking the vicar? Would you give him a ring Colin? Ask him to call round to old Charlie's, to see what's happened."

"Tell you what, Dad, I'll go and get him." Colin glanced out at the sloping shadows and the bright sky. It was still quite a long time to sunset. "I won't be long, I promise."

And he was out of the door before his parents could stop him.

Chapter two

Colin liked the vicar. Colin, Joy, Mum and Dad all went down to the family service on Sundays. Colin went to a group at the church on Wednesdays. Simon, the vicar, was good fun. He sometimes came to take a school assembly and would help with almost anything. Colin ran all the way to the main road and met Simon at the corner. He'd been visiting poor old Mrs Roberts who couldn't get out of her wheelchair.

"Hi, Colin," said Simon. "Where you off to?"

"To find you," said Colin, breathing heavily because he had been running very fast. "Dad said I was to tell you… there's a dog, and she's ever so thin… I think she's starving… and the house looks all shut up. Will and I were feeding her, but—"

"Who does this dog belong to?" asked Simon.

"Dad says she belongs to old Charlie," said Colin. "Dad says you'd best call round."

"Old Charlie?" said Simon. 'I know him but he doesn't like being called on. He's never let me into the house… Well, let's go and have a look."

Colin and Simon climbed the steep lane and turned up the track. It was getting dark in the oak wood and Colin was glad he was not alone. It would soon be sunset but there were no lights in the cottage windows. They stood at the gate and whistled. The dog came rushing to them, whining and pushing her nose through the gate. When the vicar pushed it open she jumped up barking. But she knew Colin and when he got hold of her she quietened down and wagged her tail.

"Feel her ribs," said Colin, stroking her gently.

The vicar knocked on the front door. There was no answer. He went round to the back. There was a pile of bricks against a rain barrel. The dog jumped up and started drinking.

"At least she's had water," said Simon.

He knocked at the back door. Then he tried to open the door but it was locked.

He peered in through the windows. "I don't think there's anyone here," he said. "Old Charlie must have gone away. I'd better phone the police and ask them to look into it. In the meantime…"

"I'll look after her," said Colin.

"Well, it would be best to take her home," said Simon. "Would your mum and dad mind?"

"I don't think so," said Colin.

"Well, I'm sure we can sort her out in a day or two," said the vicar. "She'll just be a lodger."

"Not if I can help it," said Colin. "If anything's happened to old Charlie, I'm keeping her."

"Well, we'll see," smiled the vicar. "Take her home now and give her a good supper. Tell your dad I'll look after old Charlie. Bye, Colin, and thanks."

"Thanks a lot," called Colin. He kept tight hold of the dog's collar but she didn't struggle. She seemed glad to follow her new master. They climbed the hill together. When they reached the top, the sun was setting. The farm and the barns stood black against a crimson sky. They reached the house and Colin pushed open the door. The dog walked straight into the big farm kitchen. She began poking her

nose into cupboards and whining. The family's cat arched her back, hissed and ran out into the yard.

"Oh, that's the dog, is it? You know, I had a feeling you'd come back with her!" said Mum. "Did you find old Charlie?"

"No," said Colin. "Simon came and he thinks the house is empty. He's going to phone the police. He told me to bring the dog home, and if old Charlie's gone away or something, I can keep her."

"*Keep* her?" Mum looked doubtful. "We've already got a dog! I don't know what your dad will say… Still, she's here now and you'd best feed her.'

She found an old bowl. Colin opened a tin of dog food and threw in a handful of dog biscuits. The black dog trembled with excitement and wagged her tail furiously.

She seemed to finish the meal in one great gulp and whined for more.

"That's enough for now," said Mum. "You've already fed her this afternoon. Give her some water and let her be."

Colin sat down on the mat beside the dog. She laid her head on his lap and fell asleep. He stayed very still for a long time, stroking her. Then Dad came in for a drink and a cheese sandwich. Joy joined them,

grumbling about her homework. But mostly they talked about old Charlie and the sleeping dog.

"Dad, if he's gone away or dead or something, can I keep her?"

"That's not fair," said Joy. "She ought to belong to both of us. She's smaller than Growler and much more friendly. I like her."

But Colin shook his head. "If you want another dog, you get one for yourself," he said. "This one's mine… just mine."

"Bedtime, Colin," said Mum quickly, fearing an argument. "Mind you wash properly! And don't be too sure about keeping the dog till we've found out about old Charlie. Anyhow, we haven't said you *can* keep her, even if—"

"Oh, Dad, I can, can't I?" cried Colin.

Dad's mouth was full but he looked straight at Colin. Colin looked straight at Dad. Dad winked; Colin hugged him and went up to bed.

But not to sleep. Dad had to be up milking at half past four and he and Mum went to bed soon after Colin. Colin waited until he heard them come upstairs and shut their bedroom door. Joy was in her room, finishing her homework.

Colin crept downstairs on silent bare feet. The dog whined, lifted her head and pawed his knees. "You're lonely in this strange place," whispered Colin. "You can come and sleep with me tonight."

When Mum went to wake Colin for school next morning, she nearly exploded with rage. Colin lay fast asleep with his head on the pillow. And, snuggled up

against him with *her* head on the pillow,
lay the dog.

Chapter three

When Colin came out of school next day, the vicar was waiting for him and walked down the road with him.

"Well?" said Simon. "What about that dog?"

"She's fine. Dad says I can keep her. Well… he *sort* of said so. What about old Charlie?"

"We've found out about him. The police got in and found the house empty. But there was a letter from his sister in Ledbury and they phoned her. Charlie went on the bus to spend the day with her last Saturday. He was taken ill and rushed into hospital. He didn't know anything till last night, but now he's coming round.

First thing he did was ask about the dog. I said not to worry, she was in good hands."

"That's right. But will old Charlie come home?"

"I doubt it. He's had a stroke and his sister thinks he'll have to stay in hospital. If he hears the dog's in a good home, I think he'll be glad to leave it at that."

Colin stood still in the middle of the road and looked at the vicar. "Then she's mine now?" he asked.

"Seems like it," said the vicar.

"Then you tell old Charlie she'll have a good home all right," said Colin. "I'd best get back and see how she's doing. Can I bring her to Wednesday group?"

"Er… I suppose so," said the vicar rather doubtfully. "As long as they don't *all* want to bring dogs. We'll see how it goes."

"Thanks," sai~~d~~ Friend
quickly, up the lane. He re~~a~~ct off, very
very out of breath and met his dad going
to the milking shed.

"She's mine, Dad," he puffed, "mine to
keep."

"Who is?"

... Charlie's in hospital and
"The not coming back. I can keep her.
Oh Dad, I *can* keep her, can't I?"

"Well, I suppose so. But she's to sleep in the kitchen and that's that. Understand? Your mum was very upset when she found her on your bed."

Colin grinned, and ran to the house. The dog came, barking, to meet him. He flung his arms round her neck. "You're mine! And I'm going to call you Friska," he

whispered. "I'll let Joy take you out for a walk sometimes but you're mine, mine, mine."

But poor Joy didn't get much of a chance to walk Friska. Friska would follow no one but Colin. The dog howled when Colin went to school and rushed down the lane to meet him when he came home. On Saturday he walked her far across the fields and woods and on Sunday he wanted to take her to church.

"The vicar wouldn't mind," said Colin. "She was ever so good at Wednesday group."

"Don't be silly, Colin," said Mum. Friska whined and Joy started laughing. "You'll have her in the music group with me next!" she said.

"Now come on, and stop fooling," said Dad. They set off down the lane and when they reached the road, Joy began to run. She wanted to see her friends in the music group before the service began.

Everyone in the village liked the vicar and the church was nearly full for the family service. Colin usually enjoyed the first part – all the songs – but he and the other young people went off to their Bible classes then. So he did not often listen to the sermon. But today was different. Simon read a verse from the Bible twice through and then made the children say it after him. The vicar told them that this was what God said: "Don't be afraid. I have rescued you. I have called you by name; now you belong to me."

And then – Colin could hardly believe it! Simon was talking about him… but he did not say his name.

"This week," said Simon, "a sad thing happened to old Mr Brown who lived on the edge of the common. But it would have been much sadder if it had not been for two kind boys."

Colin blushed.

The vicar went on to talk about the hungry, lonely dog and how two boys had noticed and cared about it. (At this point, Colin turned his head and grinned at Will.) Simon told how he and one of the boys had whistled at the gate and how the dog had come rushing out. Then he told the people what Colin had said: "Then she's mine now … she'll have a good home all right."

Simon went on to say how the dog had come to Wednesday group but would go to no one but her own master. "He's named her Friska," said the vicar. "He only

has to call her name and the dog runs to him. She isn't lonely or hungry or frightened any more. She's his, and I know he'll care for her."

Colin smiled at Dad and nudged Mum.

"And it was this," said the vicar, "that reminded me of the verse we just read in the Bible." He went on to explain that God called people to come to him. They could say no or they could say yes. If they said yes, it was like they were answering his call, like Friska did. Like Friska, they would belong to a master who would love them and care for them. They'd belong to someone who would say to them, "Don't be afraid. I have rescued you. I have called you by name; now you belong to me."

"That's what God says to each one of us," said Simon. "He says, 'If you answer and come to me, you will be mine for ever, and safe for ever.'"

There was more, but Colin was so excited that he didn't listen much to the rest of it. When it was over, Joy came over to him, looking quite proud.

"Fancy having a sermon all about *you*, Colin!" she said very loudly.

The people nearby looked at him.

"Well, well!" said the man who ran the garage. "Well done, lad!"

And Colin's teacher said, "So *you* were the hero of the story, were you?"

Colin went redder than ever. But he did not hang around for long, for up at the farm, his dog was waiting for him. He left Mum, Dad and Joy talking outside the church and hurried up the lane.

But as he ran, part of the verse he'd heard kept going round and round in his head. He wanted to get home and say it to Friska.

"Don't be afraid. … I have called you by name; now you belong to me."

Chapter four

Old Charlie never came back. He went to live in a home near to his sister. So Friska stayed at the farm. Colin could hardly remember the time when Friska hadn't been there. She waited for him at the bottom of the stairs in the morning. She saw him off to school. She scampered down the lane to meet him on his return. She was a beautiful, glossy, bright-eyed dog now. And she was so well-behaved that no one at the farm was sorry that they had taken her in.

The summer holidays came. Colin helped his dad, and wandered over the countryside with Will and Friska. At the beginning of August the boys went to camp. Joy promised to look after Friska. It was a great week. But when the last day came, Colin could hardly wait to get back to his dog. He was nearly knocked over by her welcome.

September arrived and it was time to go back to school. The leaves were beginning to turn yellow and the hills were hidden by mists in the morning. The plums and apples were ripening in the orchard. One Saturday afternoon, Joy and Colin decided to go looking for blackberries.

"If you go down toward the hop yard they'll be best," said Mum. "Blackberries ripen quicker down in the valley."

The children ran down the rutted track that led to the distant hop fields on the further side of the farm. To the left lay the orchards but on the right the woods came down to the track. Here the hedges were heavy with blackberries. Joy and Colin

picked the juicy berries. Friska ran into the
woods to hunt for rabbits.

Suddenly they heard a furious barking.
Colin, spilling half his berries, dashed in
among the trees. He saw Friska standing
in front of a huge Alsatian dog. It was on

a leash and was growling deep in its throat. Colin grabbed Friska's collar.

The big Alsatian was being firmly held by two boys a little older than himself. They wore scruffy clothes and one carried a sack over his back. Neither they nor the dog looked very friendly. Colin felt a bit scared. He made for the edge of the wood, dragging Friska behind him. She was still barking.

Joy had climbed the bank to see what was going on. She wasn't afraid of the boys with the big dog. She smiled.

"Hi," she said.

"All right?" said the eldest of the boys. The big dog stopped growling. Friska stopped barking. And Colin stopped feeling afraid.

Then Joy asked them what they'd got in their sack.

"Want to see?" said the older boy. He opened the sack and pulled out a pink-eyed, yellow-toothed ferret. It had dirty white fur. He pushed it toward Joy. "Let me introduce you to Rats," he said.

Joy said, "You've been rabbiting, haven't you? How many did you catch?"

"None. Swagger here's not much good at rabbiting." The older boy looked at his dog. "He's too big."

"That's a nice-looking little dog you've got there," said the younger boy, pointing at Friska. "Want to sell it?"

"No way," said Colin quickly. It was such a terrible idea that he put his arms round Friska and held her tight.

The younger boy said no more. He just glared, his dark curls half over his eyes.

"Where d'you live, then?" the older boy asked Joy.

"Up at the farm on the hill. Where do you live?"

"In a better house than yours. Want to see?"

"Yes, OK," said Joy. "How far is it?"

"Just down by the road in the lay-by."

Joy and Colin looked at each other. Colin didn't really want to go but he could see Joy did. He couldn't let her go alone so he gave a little nod.

"Come on then," said the older boy.

They went down the track until they came to the main road. A van was parked in the lay-by hitched to a trailer – a long, white caravan with scarlet curtains. A group of people sat round outside, talking and laughing. The children stopped a little way off.

"There," said the older boy proudly. "Good, isn't it? These are my people." He nodded towards his friend. "*His* people live in another trailer. It'll be along soon."

"It's great," said Joy. "I wish I lived in a house like that! Where are you going?"

"Dunno… on to the hops somewhere. Might be anywhere," said the older boy. "Want to see inside?"

"Not now, we must go back," said Joy.

"OK," said the older boy. "Cheers then." He smiled in a friendly way but the younger boy still said nothing. He just stared and his bright eyes were fixed on Friska.

Joy and Colin hurried up the track, talking about the caravan. They thought it must be wonderful to live in a trailer, always moving on. That kind of life made the farm seem quite boring.

It was dusk and rabbits were coming out in the twilight. Friska kept rushing into the woods and the children did not wait for her. She often chased rabbits and she knew her way home.

They arrived back happy and hungry. Mum was cooking tea. There was a lovely smell in the kitchen. Joy and Colin sat down with glasses of orange juice. They told Mum all about their adventure and

how they wished they lived in a caravan. Mum laughed and said she was happy on the farm.

"Where's Friska?" said Colin suddenly. "I wonder if she's caught a rabbit for a change. She hardly ever does. She makes too much noise."

"Let her be," said Mum. "A dog wants to have a bit of fun on its own. She'll come in her own time."

Colin went to the door and stood looking out at the darkening hills. A new moon hung behind the woods and an owl hooted. He felt a bit jealous thinking about Friska having fun on her own without him. He whistled.

There was no answer. The owl hooted again. Colin stepped out into the yard and looked round. Friska must be having a very exciting time to stay out so long. He

walked a little way to where the woods came down to the edge of the track.

"Friska!" he called. "Good dog! Come home now. Good dog!"

But there was still no Friska. The leaves rustled and some little animals ran about in a ditch... just the ordinary night sounds. No happy barking or scampering paws. Colin suddenly felt very scared. He rushed back to the house. He was glad to find his father in the kitchen.

"Dad! Mum! Joy!" he shouted. "Friska's not there! She never goes far. She always comes when I call. She's gone!"

"Let's *all* call," said Joy, and they all ran outside. Up and down the track they went, calling and calling. They went all the way back to the place where they had picked blackberries. Then they came all the way back home, still calling. But it was no good. Friska had completely disappeared.

"We'll have to go home now, Colin," said Dad sadly. "Maybe someone's stolen her. We might have to ring the police."

They went back into the kitchen and Dad put his arm round Colin's shoulders. Colin began to cry.

"We'll find her, son," he said. "Maybe she'll come home in the night. We'll hear if she scratches."

Joy looked up suddenly. "Cal," she said, "do you think that boy could have taken her? The younger one? He wanted to buy her and he kept looking at her."

Colin gave a big sniff. "But she was with us till we were nearly home," he said. "I saw her chase a rabbit into the woods just below the crab apple tree."

"The boy could have followed us," said Joy. "It was getting dark and we were hurrying. We didn't look round."

Colin got quite excited. "Then the police could find him," he said. "We know what the caravan looks like, white with red curtains."

Joy shook her head. "That one belonged to the older boy's family," she said. "The other one was waiting for the trailer to arrive. We didn't see it. But we'd know Friska anywhere. It ought to be easy."

"We'll get the police first thing tomorrow morning," said Dad.

Colin drank a cup of tea and went up to bed very quietly. His mother looked in later and thought he was asleep. His father only discovered their mistake next morning. He came downstairs, yawning,

and found Colin asleep in his sleeping bag… right by the door.

Chapter five

It was a sad rainy morning. Colin came in late to breakfast, cold and wet and very miserable. He had been up early, searching the woods. He thought perhaps Friska had been hurt, but Dad shook his head.

"We'd have heard her howling," he said. "I think Joy's right and she's gone with the hop pickers. I'll ring the police."

But the police were not very hopeful. The hop fields were spread out all over the county and Colin probably hadn't seen the right trailer. They had to have a warrant to search caravans. They said every caravan had one or two dogs and their owners would probably say they'd had them since they were puppies. They said that if a dog was stolen, it would most likely be tied up inside a van and only let out at night. Still, they told Colin's dad that they'd have a look round.

"Well," said Mum, "we'd best get ready for church. Colin, would you rather stop home? I don't suppose the dog will come but you never know."

Colin hesitated. He somehow felt that he would like to see the vicar. Simon had been really helpful in tracking down old Charlie. The vicar always seemed to have good ideas when things went wrong. But if Friska came back, Colin did not want her to come home to an empty house. He decided to stay.

"But tell Simon why," he said. "He'll want to know about Friska."

But there was no sign of Friska. Colin wandered about the yard or sat in the kitchen window. The time seemed to pass

very slowly. At last he heard Joy clatter up the steps and fling open the door.

"The vicar's coming, Cal," she announced breathlessly. "He's coming specially to see you."

Colin ran to the window. Sure enough, Mum, Dad and Simon were coming across the yard. The vicar had changed from his church clothes into an old jacket and wellington boots. Colin jumped the steps and met him.

"Did they tell you?" he said. "She's gone. Dad and Joy think it might be the hop pickers, but she might be hurt somewhere…"

"Well, let's check she's not hurt. We'll have one more search round," said Simon. "The sun's coming out. Look, there's a rainbow over the hills. Have you been round to old Charlie's place?"

Colin shook his head.

"Let's try there first then," said the vicar.

Outside, the rainbow grew brighter and brighter and all the world looked clean and shining. They searched the woods right up to the ridge and down the other side. They went to Charlie's house which was a wilderness of weeds and nettles. They sat down on the rough log beneath

the window. Colin was quite tired and very miserable.

"Supposing Friska's hurt," he said. "Or supposing she's gone with that boy. Perhaps she's hungry. Perhaps he'll beat her. And she won't like being shut in a caravan. Friska's an outdoor dog."

"Oh, I'm sure the boy would be kind to her," said the vicar. "Listen, Colin, do you ever pray about things?"

Colin nodded. "I say my prayers at night. I say, 'Our Father in heaven, help us to honour your name...' I can't remember the rest of that prayer. Anyway, then I say, 'Bless Mum and Dad and Joy and me' and last night I said, 'Bless Friska'."

"Well, that's a good prayer. But do you believe there really is a Father in heaven? Do you think you can belong to him, tell him everything and ask him to help you?"

Colin frowned. He had never really thought about it.

"Dunno," he said.

"Well, when you do believe he's really there, it makes things all different. Do you remember the verse you learned when I told the story of you and your dog?"

Colin smiled. "'Don't be afraid. … ' I can't remember the middle bit. Then it went, 'I have called you by name; now you belong to me.'" I said it to Friska when I got home."

The vicar laughed. "You said it to Friska, but God says it to you! 'Don't be afraid, Colin. I have rescued you. I have called you by name; now you belong to me.'"

"What does it mean, 'rescued'?" asked Colin. "Rescued from what?"

"Colin, you know God is good. He loves us and wants us to belong to him. But sometimes we don't listen to him. We go the wrong way and do wrong things. But when Jesus came, he said, 'I'll take away those wrong things and put you right with God.'"

"How did he do that?" asked Colin.

"He took the punishment we all deserve for doing wrong when he died on the cross. He paid the price. He rescued us. Now he calls us to be his children, and you can say yes or no. It's best to say yes. When you belong to God, then you have a loving heavenly Father. You can tell him everything and you need never feel lonely or scared. You can tell him about Friska and ask him to help you find her. He loves us and he wants to help – he's always there for us. And Colin, remember: he doesn't always give us exactly what we ask for. But he always does the thing that is right and best."

"It would be right and best to find Friska," said Colin. "Could you ask him now?"

So they prayed and asked God to look after Friska, wherever she was, and to bring her back. Then they left the cottage and said goodbye. Colin went home feeling much happier. If God was really so great, he must know where Friska was and he would look after her.

Chapter six

The week passed slowly. The police said they were still keeping their eyes open but so far they had seen nothing of a black mongrel dog. Every day Colin hurried back from school with just a tiny hope in his heart that Friska might come rushing to meet him. But there was no sound except the cows, mooing as they went to the milking, or Growler's deep bark. Growler was a big dog who guarded the yard and he wasn't very friendly. But he seemed to know Colin was upset. He licked Colin's hand and pretended to be a gentle dog. Colin would sometimes cry into his bristly coat and bring him extra dog biscuits.

On Saturday morning, Colin woke very early. Dad was in the barn and the house was silent. It was a clear day with golden leaves blowing about. Sprays of crimson creeper waved in the wind. Colin leaned on the sill and suddenly knew what he was going to do that day. He would have one last try. After all, Friska must be somewhere. He thought of waking Joy and asking her to go with him. But then he remembered she had to go back to school for a hockey match.

He dressed and went to the kitchen. He found some food – a bread roll, an apple and some pork pie. He put on his wellingtons. He was ready to set off and no one must stop him. He wouldn't tell his mum and dad in case they tried to talk him out of it. He'd just write a note and go.

So he started off down the track. He went past the crab apple tree and the orchards. He went past the blackberry

hedges. Then he came to the road and the lay-by where the van and its trailer had parked. It had been heading north toward Worcester and there were hop yards all the way.

"Who knows?" he said to himself. "I might turn out to be a good detective. I might even be one when I grow up."

He trotted along as the warm September sun rose in the sky. He was going down a road where a fluffy plant called old man's beard grew. There were also bright red rose hips in the hedges. Behind the hedges, the hop yards stretched away as far as he could see. But there were no caravans – only little clusters of sheds where the pickers who didn't have caravans bedded down. Colin went as close to these as he dared and watched for a long time. But they were mostly locked and deserted, for the people were all out working in the fields. There were no dogs about.

He began to get very tired and sat down under a tree to eat his lunch. He kept back some pork pie in case he found Friska. The sun was almost overhead now and he knew that he would soon come to a village. He knew that because he had sometimes driven there with his dad. He also knew that there was a shop. He felt very thirsty and was thrilled to find some

change in his pocket. He could buy something to drink.

The village came in sight at last. He trailed into the shop looking hot and dusty. The shopkeeper was a kind woman and let him sit on an empty bottle case to drink the Coke he bought. The shop was almost empty and the lady was chatty. So Colin told her all about Friska and asked

her whether she knew of any caravans parked nearby.

"Well, there's three or four parked on the common through the village," she said. "But you be careful. What do you think you're going to do if you see your dog?"

"I'll call her by name," said Colin. "She'll come to me straight away."

"And maybe there will be others who'll come as well," said the woman. "Don't you do any such thing! If you see your dog, you go straight home and call your parents. They shouldn't have let you come all this way alone… you're just a kid."

"What are the hop pickers like?" said Colin.

"There's good and bad, much the same as anyone else. Some are really nice, some are really rough. But they won't take kindly to you walking off with what they think is their dog. Look, if you run up against any trouble, you come right back here, OK?"

"OK."

Colin set off past the cottages and oast houses. He walked until he could see the vans and trailers on the common. There was quite a group of them, one behind the other. He moved a little nearer and then stopped. The last caravan but one was long and white and had scarlet curtains. Colin knew it at once. There was another caravan parked just beyond it. The hop pickers, who had come in for their lunch, were sitting round on steps and benches drinking from mugs. Right in the middle of the group was a large Alsatian dog.

Chapter seven

There was an old stone wall at the edge of the common and Colin crouched behind it. He could not see much but he knew that he would have to wait. This was the pickers' lunch hour. Later, he supposed, they would go back to the fields, leaving the big dog to guard the camp. One thing he had noticed, though – the animal was on a chain.

If he could creep round to the back of the last caravan without the dog seeing him, he could at least whisper at the keyhole. If he was guessing right, that caravan belonged to the younger boy's family – the boy who had had his eye on Friska. If the boys' families had travelled together they had probably camped

together. If Friska was in there, he would only have to whisper. She would know his voice at once. He wasn't sure what he would do after that. He would have to wait and see.

He waited for a long time. He felt very small and alone. Big clouds came and hid the sun. Now and again he stood up and peered round the wall. The pickers had gone back, one by one, to the fields. At last only one old woman remained, nursing a baby. And, of course, there was the big dog.

Now his moment had come and he felt very frightened. If only he hadn't come alone! If only Dad or the vicar or even Joy were with him. He remembered that Sunday when he and Simon had searched the woods and sat on the rough log outside old Charlie's cottage. It had been a shining morning and earlier on there had been a great rainbow. He stood still, remembering what they had talked about. "Don't be afraid. ... " Then that middle bit he always forgot... and then "I have called you by name; now you belong to me."

He tried to recall what the vicar had said about that verse. What had Simon talked about? Oh yes, thought Colin, I remember. The Father in heaven calls us to be his children… we can say yes or no… if we say yes, then we're his and we need never feel lonely or afraid. He'll always be there loving us, helping us… yes, that's it. And then Colin knew he had to pray.

"Dear God," he whispered, "my name's Colin and I'm saying yes. I want to be yours. Please help me now and don't let me be so scared."

It was very quiet; the sun shone out suddenly from behind a big grey cloud. Up

in a mountain ash tree, scarlet against the orange berries, a robin sang. The sun made everything look bright and the robin's song was clear, brave and happy. Perhaps that's God answering me, thought Colin. I'll go ahead.

He tiptoed across the common, and skirted around the camp, until he was hidden out of sight behind the vans and trailers at the far end. Then he crept toward them. The old woman and the dog were hidden by the last two caravans. They could not see Colin and he could not see them.

When he reached the shelter of the last caravan, he crouched down. Then he waited for a long time, just listening. Once or twice he thought he heard a scuffling movement inside. If Friska was there, he

was surprised that she could not hear the loud beating of his heart.

Then he took a deep breath and did it. Creeping round the corner of the caravan, he crouched against the steps and put his mouth to the crack below the door.

"Friska!" he called, as loudly as he dared. "Friska, good dog! It's me, Colin…"

He got no further. It sounded as though something had suddenly exploded inside the caravan. There was a mad rush of paws and a frantic barking. Then there was the sound of furniture being knocked over and the hurtling of a body against the door. At the same time, the big Alsatian began barking too. Then Colin heard the old woman call out. A man appeared in the gap that led to the hop yards. He began to shout. Colin ran as he had never run before, dodging from caravan to caravan, streaking across the common and back to the wall. But he knew that if they ran after him, they would find him behind the wall. He must go further. So he ran uphill to where a beech tree grew with spreading roots and low boughs. It seemed made for him. He jumped, scrambled and started to climb, hand over hand, high up into the shelter of the thinner branches. No Alsatian could reach him now! He snuggled against the trunk until he got his breath back, and then peeped out through the veil of golden leaves.

Everything was spread out below him. He could see the yellow bracken on the common and the hop poles stretching away toward the sky. Not far off was the cluster of vans and trailers. Blue smoke was rising from a bonfire and people were moving about. Behind him he could see the roofs and chimneys of the village and the road winding home. Then everything went quiet again. The hop pickers went back to work and there was no sign of the Alsatian. Colin breathed a great sigh of relief, rested his cheek against the smooth bark and closed his eyes. He'd found

Friska! She was there, in the last caravan, and Dad or the police would find her.

Then he noticed something else. The shadows were growing longer. The day was getting shorter. He had been out a very long time. He shinned down the tree but he did not dare appear on the road. He crept along behind brambles and gorse bushes until he was right at the edge of the village. Then he ran to the shop.

The lady on the checkout looked up in surprise as the little boy with scratched hands and a dirty face walked in.

"What happened?" she cried.

"Found her!" said Colin. "At least, I know where she is."

"Good for you. What are you going to do now? "

"Fetch my dad; could I phone him?'"

"Sure; know his number?"

Colin nodded. Mum answered the phone and when she heard his voice she sounded very cross.

"Where *are* you, Colin? Your dad's been searching the county for you. He's been asking at all the camps and nobody has seen you. We were just about to call the police. How could you do such a thing?"

Colin was quite surprised. "But I told you, Mum," he said. "I said I was going to look for Friska. Mum, I've found her!"

"Found her?"

"Yes, but I haven't got her yet. I'm in the village shop in Leigh. Tell Dad to come at once! It's very important."

"I'll ring him. Just stop where you are, Colin, and your dad'll come."

So Colin stopped and the lady gave him crisps and Coke. He stood at the window, watching for his dad. And when there were no customers, he talked to the lady about Friska. Then, the old farm van rattled up and Dad burst into the shop.

"Where's the lad?" he asked breathlessly, looking round. Then he saw Colin and spoke quite angrily. "Don't you ever do a thing like that again, Colin! You scared the life out of your mum! Now what's all this about the dog? Your mum said you'd found her."

Colin nodded. He wasn't scared. He knew his dad was only angry because he loved him and had been worried about him.

"She's in the last caravan on the common," he said. "You've got to come and get her with me! But you'll have to be careful of the big Alsatian."

"Your son is quite a detective!" said the lady.

Dad smiled. And Colin knew that Dad was actually quite proud of him. Colin thanked the lady very politely for all her help. He promised to bring Friska to visit her another day. Then he turned to his father.

"Come on, Dad," he said. "Friska will think I've gone away and forgotten her."

Chapter eight

They got into the van and drove straight to the camp. Dad parked on the common and he and Colin walked toward the caravans. The light was beginning to fade and the hop pickers were coming from the yards. A large strong-looking man was working on the last van. His arms were covered with grease and motor oil. But Dad was large and strong too and he went up to him.

"Evening, mate," he said pleasantly. "There seems to have been a bit of a mix-up. I believe you've got my lad's dog in the trailer. Can we have a look? It's a black mongrel."

The man looked Dad full in the face. "See that dog?" he said, pointing to the large Alsatian. "He's the only one we've got. If I let him off the chain you'd best run for it. He doesn't like strangers."

They stood facing each other. Colin felt Dad give him a little push and he understood what *that* meant. He darted to the steps and called at the top of his voice.

"Friska! It's Colin. Good dog, Friska, good dog!"

Once again there was a sudden explosion and the caravan seemed to rock. Friska was hurling herself against the door over and over again, barking and scratching with all her might. The Alsatian strained at its chain and barked furiously. A crowd of pickers came running up. Then a woman's shrill voice cried, "Let the dog out, can't you, before she smashes all the china!"

A boy ran forward and opened the door and Friska sprang out with a force that made the crowd fall backwards. "Friska!" shouted Colin again and she turned and leaped on him, knocking him down.

Then Colin got up and laughed. Friska stood on her hind legs, put her paws on her master's shoulders, licked his face and wagged her tail.

Another boy ran forward. "Meg!" he called loudly. "Meg, come here."

Colin glanced at him. He had dark curls half over his eyes. Colin recognised him. It was the younger boy that he'd seen before. Friska took not the slightest notice of that boy. Then she turned and growled at the big man who had been looking on in silence. He suddenly chuckled.

"Meg," he said. "Meg indeed!" He looked at the boy with the curls. "You wait till I get my hands on you, son!"

Colin's dad stepped forward. "Look, mate," he said. "We don't want the police in on this. There's another fortnight of picking and you won't want to shift yet. My lad's been breaking his heart over that dog. Maybe your boy thought she was lost, or maybe he didn't, but that's not a problem. I'm willing to pay for the dog anyway. Take this and let's be going and good luck to you."

The man held out his hand and there was a rustle of money. "Cheers," he said, "and good luck to you and your lad."

Dad and Colin walked back to the van with Friska bounding beside them. They drove through the village in silence because Colin was too happy to speak. Then as they sped up the country road that led home, Colin said, "Dad, did you pay a lot to get her back?"

"Yes," said Dad. "She's a good dog and worth it." He rumpled Colin's hair. "Taking you all round, you're not a bad lad either."

"But she was ours already. Why should we pay for her?"

"Well, I didn't want a fuss, not with that crowd. Besides, she got away, didn't she? You must keep a close eye on her in future, Col, especially at hopping time."

They were silent again. Now they could see the farm on the hill ahead of them, black against the last glow. Colin could see the warm light streaming from the kitchen window. He was longing to tell Dad all about his great day, but he thought he'd wait until they were all together.

"Dad," he said suddenly, "it's like what the vicar was talking about. That bit from the Bible – the second part of that verse I always forget. It says, 'Don't be afraid. I have rescued you.'"

"Eh? Oh, yes," said Dad. "Jesus bought us back from bad things when he died for us. And I bought Friska back. Yes, Cal, I see what you mean." Then he frowned. "Listen, Colin, if your mum tells you off, remember you deserve it. You never ought to have gone off on your own like that, scaring her stiff.

Indoors, Mum had meant to be cross, but she couldn't. She was too pleased to see Colin – and Friska – home and safe. And, when she heard the whole story, she was proud of Colin being so brave. Colin was so tired he only just managed to tell the story (and eat a big plate of sausage and chips) before he fell asleep. He was happy to go to bed because he knew when he woke up in the morning he'd find Friska in her basket by the cooker.

He was up early next day and he and Friska ran out into the cool, misty morning. The grass was covered with spiders' webs. They went across the fields and chased about in the grass. Colin always took Friska for a run on Sunday mornings because she had to stay behind

when they went to church. He especially wanted to go to church that morning because he wanted to tell the vicar all about his great adventure. So the moment the service was over, Colin rushed up to him.

"Hey, Simon," he said, grabbing his sleeve, "you know Friska was lost? Well, I went and found her. I went all by myself all the way to Leigh and I saw the caravans and…"

"Just a moment," said the vicar. "This is too good to hurry. I'll go and shake hands with the people. You ask your mum if you can come over to the vicarage. Then you can tell me all about it."

So Joy promised to tell Friska that Colin wouldn't be long. About twenty minutes later, Colin and the vicar sat down in the vicarage sitting room. Simon's wife

brought some juice and biscuits and she and their baby listened to the story too. And when Colin had finished, he said, "And you know, Simon, it was like the second bit of that verse. The bit I forget! We rescued Friska. Dad bought her back. He said it's like what Jesus did on the cross. Friska needed rescuing so Dad paid the price to do it. We need rescuing from bad things, too, don't we? And Jesus did it."

"Yes, Colin. That's right," said Simon.

"And when I was sitting behind the wall I was scared and I said yes."

The vicar blinked. "What do you mean?"

"Well, when we get scared, God's there for us, isn't he, when we belong to him? That's what you said. God calls us by our name and we can say yes or no, and I said yes. It was as though God said, 'You belong to me.' And then I wasn't so scared any more. Friska wasn't scared when I called her by name. She came bounding out and then she belonged to me again. But Dad had to pay for her and she cost him a lot."

"Well done, Colin," said the vicar. "You've really understood. 'Don't be afraid. I have rescued you.' What your dad said was right. You had to be bought back too, Colin, before you could belong to God. Just like Friska got into the wrong hands, so we fall into the hands of bad stuff and wrong things. We tell lies and are selfish and lose our tempers. Think about it, Colin — if lies and arguing went into heaven, it wouldn't be heaven any longer, would it? So we need to be rescued from all that bad stuff so we can belong to God."

Colin looked thoughtful.

"That's why Jesus came. He died on the cross and was punished instead of us for the wrong things we had done. He paid for them instead of us so now we can be forgiven and belong to God again. So we're rescued and bought back for God," said Simon.

Colin listened and nodded his head. "That's why people love Jesus so much,

Simon! Because he loved us enough to suffer so much."

Simon smiled. "You've got it!"

Colin stood up. "I must get back to Friska. But yes, Simon, I do get it. 'Don't be afraid. I have rescued you. I have called you by name; now you belong to me.' I can say it to Friska and God has said it to me."

He thought about it as he walked up the lane, scuffling through the golden leaves that had already started to fall. He felt very happy. He had shown Friska how much he loved her. He'd walked all that way. He'd braved the big Alsatian dog and the hop pickers. He'd crept up to the caravan and called her by name. He'd rescued her... she'd been bought back. And he knew Friska would always love him.

But Jesus had done far more than Colin had done for his dog. Jesus had died on the cross and suffered a lot of pain to rescue Colin.

I love him too, thought Colin. I'm glad I said yes. I'm glad I belong to God. There was a wild barking and Friska came hurtling down the lane to meet him.

"And," said Colin out loud, "I'm so very, VERY glad that Friska my friend is home again!"